Kindness

by Adam Rapp

A SAMUEL FRENCH ACTING EDITION

SAMUEL FRENCH

FOUNDED 1830

NEW YORK HOLLYWOOD LONDON TORONTO

SAMUELFRENCH.COM

ISBN 978-0-573-69680-0   Printed in U.S.A.   #29096

MUSIC NOTE

Licensees are solely responsible for obtaining formal written permission from copyright owners to use copyrighted music in the performance of this play and are strongly cautioned to do so. If no such permission is obtained by the licensee, then the licensee must use only original music that the licensee owns and controls. Licensees are solely responsible and liable for all music clearances and shall indemnify the copyright owners of the play and their licensing agent, Samuel French, Inc., against any costs, expenses, losses and liabilities arising from the use of music by licensees.

IMPORTANT BILLING AND CREDIT REQUIREMENTS

All producers of *KINDNESS* *must* give credit to the Author of the Play in all programs distributed in connection with performances of the Play, and in all instances in which the title of the Play appears for the purposes of advertising, publicizing or otherwise exploiting the Play and/or a production. The name of the Author *must* appear on a separate line on which no other name appears, immediately following the title and *must* appear in size of type not less than fifty percent of the size of the title type.

In addition the following credit must be given in all programs and publicity information distributed in association with this piece:

Playwrights Horizons, Inc.,
produced the world premiere of *KINDNESS*
Off-Broadway in 2008

KINDNESS premiered at Playwrights Horizons (Tim Sanford, artistic director) at the Peter J. Sharp Theater on Oct. 13, 2008. The performance was directed by Adam Rapp, with sets by Lauren Helpern, costumes by Daphne Javitch, lighting by Mary Louise Geiger, and sound, byEric Shim. The production stage manager was Richard A. Hodge. The cast was as follows:

DENNIS....................................Christopher Denham

MARYANNE..................................Annette O'Toole

HERMAN...................................Ray Anthony Thomas

FRANCES.................................. Katherine Waterston

CHARACTERS

Dennis
Maryanne
Herman
Frances

ACT ONE

(In the dark we hear classic porn music. We also hear a boy's voice and heavy breathing.)

(Lights up on a Midtown Manhattan Hotel Room. Two full beds, a small nightstand with a drawer between the beds, family photos on the nightstand. A curtained window. A table with a phone. A door leading to a bathroom. Next to a closet, a large desk-like table with a phone. A swivel chair pushed into the table. Over one of the beds, a large framed photo of Central Park's 107th Infantry Memorial statue hanging on the wall. An overstuffed chair positioned toward a large armoire containing a TV. On the shelf below the TV, a stuffed monkey, a Statue of Liberty paperweight and a few souvenir spoons. On the TV, two women are naked, dancing, and sharing an apple. Seated in the overstuffed chair and masturbating as if his life depends on it is DENNIS, 17. He is white, thin, pasty, boyishly handsome. He sports a short military academy hair cut, though it is not a crew cut, and wears Adidas basketball warm-up pants, high top basketball sneakers, and a hoody. His sweat pants are down at his ankles and he is nearing completion. He counts down from ten. Near blast-off he cries "I'm coming! I'm coming! Mohammed Ali!" The front door opens. DENNIS grabs the first thing he can find, covers his lap, and orgasms thoroughly. His mother, MARYANNE, late forties, a little out of breath, somehow lost, walks in. She walks with a cane. Somehow DENNIS switches the channel on the TV. An excruciatingly embarrassing situation for him, though it doesn't quite register with MARYANNE.)

DENNIS. Ma!

MARYANNE. Were you just callin my name, Dennis?

DENNIS. What?! No!

MARYANNE. Are you sure?

DENNIS. I wasn't callin your name.

MARYANNE. Well, that's strange. I coulda sworn I heard you really callin out to me. I thought maybe there was some sorta terrible crisis…Whatcha wathcin?

DENNIS. What's it look like I'm watchin?

MARYANNE. A friggin Lucky Charms commercial, don't be a smart-ass.

DENNIS. I'm watchin the Knicks.

MARYANNE. Who are they playin?

DENNIS. Orlando.

MARYANNE. Whose winnin?

DENNIS. It's still in the first quarter. What are you doin back?

MARYANNE. I forgot my jacket. It suddenly got so chilly. You haven't seen it, have you? The baby blue windbreaker with the little goose on the front – the one your Aunt Billy got me for my birthday?

(He looks to his lap and realizes that he has climaxed into the very jacket.)

MARYANNE. I coulda sworn I left it in here.

*(While she looks for it, **DENNIS** manages to pull his pants up and wedges the blue jacket between him and the side of the chair. She sits in the swivel chair.)*

MARYANNE. I'm so out of breath all of the sudden.

DENNIS. Well, you know what Dr. Baron said.

MARYANNE. Oh, Dr. Baron can go jump in a lake.

DENNIS. That's mature.

MARYANNE. I'm tired of Dr. Baron. That breath of his. Those hairy ears.

DENNIS. *(turning the TV off)* You're sposed to be takin it easy.

MARYANNE. I started walkin up Seventh Avenue and I was doin pretty good. Boy, New York sure is a whirlwind of a city, Dennis. All the lights. The billboards. They got these buses that are about as long as a football field. Two, three buses all linked together. And so many people on the street. I saw a man wearin nothin but his underwear and a cowboy hat. No socks even. Some chest on that guy, too. The chest of a bullfighter. A bullfighter or maybe some typa athlete. I got all the way to Forty-Second Street when I realized I forgot my jacket.

DENNIS. You walked back?

MARYANNE. I took a cab. I had the nicest driver, too, Dennis. Just the nicest man. Struck up a conversation with me right away, askin where I'm from, was it my first time here, etcetera, etcetera. You hear about these New York City cabs with the prostitutes and unsavory types doin business in the backseat and such. This was the complete opposite of that, Dennis. The guy didn't even charge me the fare. I went to swipe my debit card in the transaction thingy and he stops me cold and says it's on the house.

DENNIS. Who was he, a priest?

MARYANNE. He was just a regular type guy. As regular as they come. He's actually waitin for me downstairs.

DENNIS. He is?

MARYANNE. He's double-parked with his hazards on, I kid you not.

DENNIS. Why?

MARYANNE. Well, I started talkin about the play and it turns out the poor guy hasn't ever seen a Broadway musical. Lived here all his life and not one musical – imagine that. That's like livin next to the aquarium and never knowin what an octopus looks like. An octopus or a barracuda or whathaveyou. And he said he's always wanted to see this particular musical cause of how he gets so many post-show fares at that exact theater and how his customers are all aglow and inspired and hummin the songs. He even knows about the subject matter and such. We talked about the themes and how they relate to life. Survivin in the streets –

DENNIS. *(smartass)* Survivin'!: *The Musical.*

MARYANNE. *(pressing on, firm)* And meetin your soul mate and the quest for human connection and dealin with bad news. And he showed genuine concern and a true depth of curiosity, Dennis. We even talked about what constitutes a good love song. I mean, in a matter of four-five blocks we had just the nicest conversation.

DENNIS. What's his name?

MARYANNE. Herman.

DENNIS. *Herman?*

MARYANNE. Yeah, what's wrong with Herman?

DENNIS. It sounds like some old guy with hemorrhoids.

MARYANNE. Hemorrhoids. You don't even know what hemorrhoids are.

DENNIS. Yes I do.

MARYANNE. Oh yeah? What are they?

DENNIS. It's when your jazzhole puckers.

MARYANNE. Your *who?*

DENNIS. Your jazzhole.

MARYANNE. What the heck is a jazzhole?

DENNIS. A jazzhole's a anus.

MARYANNE. Dennis, that's not what hemorrhoids are.

DENNIS. It is too, Ma. It's when your jazzhole puckers and you crap projectile blood. My history teacher at school has em.

MARYANNE. What history teacher?

DENNIS. Sergeant Dietz. He has hemorrhoids and herpes on his lips and he grows a mustache to try and hide it.

MARYANNE. To hide his hemorrhoids or his herpes?

DENNIS. His herpes. They're all over his upper lip.

MARYANNE. Well, that's disgusting.

DENNIS. His mustache isn't even regulation but the Commandant lets him grow it out cause it's so gross.

MARYANNE. Well, they should give him some cortisone or a special cream or somethin. God, what a mess *he* sounds like. And just for the record, smart guy, hemorrhoids are when your intestines get irritated and start pressin through your backside.

DENNIS. Same difference.

MARYANNE. It's not the same difference. It's your intestines that get irritated, not your friggin jazzthingy.

DENNIS. Jazz*hole*.

MARYANNE. Jazz*hole*. Where the heck do you come up with these phrases anyway? You and your lingo. What was it you called that nice lady at the desk, a skizzle?

DENNIS. Skeezer.

MARYANNE. Yeah, whatever that means.

DENNIS. It's classic Hi-hop, Yo.

MARYANNE. Oh, go Yo yourself.

DENNIS. A skeezer's a well-appointed woman.

MARYANNE. Yeah, a well-appointed *somethin*...Dennis, you can't go around callin people names, especially in public.

DENNIS. She didn't hear me.

MARYANNE. You don't know that for certain. And she was overweight, too.

DENNIS. What does that have to do with anything?

MARYANNE. Well, you coulda really hurt that poor woman's feelings. It's not easy for the obese. Especially these days with everyone bein so thin and attracted to themselves and all. The obese and the homeless – they're the ones who have it roughest.

DENNIS. Fine. I'm a terrible person. Shoot me in the mouth.

MARYANNE. Oh, you are not a terrible person. And stop sayin that.

DENNIS. Take me out back and shoot me in the mouth. Bust a cap in my ass.

MARYANNE. Hemorrhoids concern your intestines and you get em because of lack of fiber.

DENNIS. Yeah, you know everything.

MARYANNE. I certainly know more than you on the subject, that's for sure. Have you ever had hemorrhoids?

DENNIS. No.

MARYANNE. Well, I did. In fact, I had em when I was carryin you, Mister Classic Hip-Hop Lingo Stud Champion. I had em all through my final trimester and it's no walk in the park, let me tell you.

DENNIS. I'm sorry I ruined your perfect life.

MARYANNE. Oh, stop being dramatic. Anyway, Herman's not some old guy with hemorrhoids. In fact I might even wager that he's younger than the bag of hammers that sits before you.

DENNIS. You're not a bag of hammers.

MARYANNE. You taken a good look at me lately?

DENNIS. You look better than when you were doin chemo.

MARYANNE. I don't even know if that's true, I really don't.

(She stops suddenly doubles over in pain. She crosses to the table, brings a wadded tissue to her mouth.)

DENNIS. You okay?

(There is blood in her tissue.)

DENNIS. Maybe you should lay down.

MARYANNE. I'm fine.

*(**DENNIS** crosses to the bathroom, exits, returns with a glass of water and a hand towel.)*

DENNIS. You want the Pedialyte?

*(She shakes her head. **DENNIS** crosses to the bed closest to the window, hurls himself on to it, face-down.)*

DENNIS. So you're gonna take this guy to the play?

MARYANNE. Well, that's sorta what I wanted to discuss with you – the other ticket bein yours originally.

DENNIS. You want me to clear outta here later so you can have some privacy?

MARYANNE. Now, that's ridiculous. We'd be goin as friends.

DENNIS. He's takin you in his cab?

MARYANNE. Sure.

DENNIS. Classy.

MARYANNE. Whattaya mean, classy.

DENNIS. You're gonna roll up in a *cab?*

MARYANNE. A car's a friggin car – what the heck do I care? Since when did you become such a snob, anyway? Boy...

DENNIS. Did he ask you about your cane?

MARYANNE. I told him I have a bad ankle. I said I banged it.

DENNIS. On what?

MARYANNE. On your generally bad attitude.

DENNIS. Hardy-har.

MARYANNE. Oh, hardy-har yourself.

DENNIS. Ma, this is how people get chopped up and stuffed inna suitcase. Especially in this city.

MARYANNE. Well, that's certainly grim. You've seen too many movies.

DENNIS. What movies?

MARYANNE. You know what movies. The ones with all those moody Italians and their hysterical girlfriends. The movies by Martin Scorcese and Yancy Tarantino or whatever his name is.

DENNIS. Quentin.

MARYANNE. Yeah, Quentin Tarantino – the thugmeister himself.

DENNIS. He's not a thug, Ma. He's a regular guy. He used to work as a clerk in a video store.

MARYANNE. Oh, yeah, sure – a video clerk. That's what they'd *like* you to believe.

DENNIS. They meanin...

MARYANNE. They meanin they.

DENNIS. Qualify your pronouns please.

MARYANNE. I'll qualify somethin, all right. Get your shoes off the bed. That's where I'm sleepin!

*(**DENNIS** raises his shoes up playfully, then eventually sits up, placing his feet on the floor. He opens and closes the drawer to the bedside table a few times, then stops. Over the following, he gently knocks all the family photos down:)*

MARYANNE. For the record I just wanna say one more time how much I wanted you to see this play with me. I mean, what the heck, kiddo, we flew all the way out here, spent all of Grandpa Shoe's money on the hotel package. This nice landmark hotel. And I got you your sweat suit and we had such a nice day at Macy's and at the library and walkin around Bryant P – put those back!

*(**DENNIS** rights the picture frames.)*

MARYANNE. You promised you would come.

DENNIS. You bribed me.

MARYANNE. How did I bribe you?

DENNIS. By buyin me the sweatsuit.

MARYANNE. Dennis, I bought you the sweatsuit cause you got your grades up.

DENNIS. But you couldn't stop talkin about the play while we were in line for the register.

MARYANNE. Cause I was excited!

DENNIS. And now you're usin it against me so here...

(He removes the bottoms, throws them on the floor next to him, then goes into his travel bag, removes the top, throws that on the floor as well.)

DENNIS. Return it.

MARYANNE. Maybe I don't wanna return it.

DENNIS. Well, now I don't want it.

MARYANNE. Well, I don't want it either, so...

DENNIS. So what?

MARYANNE. So nothin, you got no pants on.

(A stale mate for a bit.)

MARYANNE. Look at the sticks on that guy.

(DENNIS doesn't respond.)

MARYANNE. You got some nice legs there, bub. I'll bet you're a ball player. How's your vertical leap? You the new white Jordan everyone's talkin about? The high-flyin Marzipan man?

(He says nothing.)

MARYANNE. Well, at least put your pants back on.

(He doesn't.)

MARYANNE. I guess I'll just have to stare at your sexy gams. The hams, the gams and the shanks, that's where the money's at.

DENNIS. Okay, Dad.

MARYANNE. Your father learned that one from me.

DENNIS. Uh-huh.

MARYANNE. He did. He learned it from me cause your Uncle Stags used to say it to your grandma to tease her...I wonder where the oaf is right now, anyway. What the heck he's up to.

DENNIS. Who, Uncle Stags?

MARYANNE. Your father.

DENNIS. You know what he's up to.

MARYANNE. Maybe he's figurin some things out.

DENNIS. *(sitting on his bed, putting his pants back on)* Ma, he's prolly at a casino, and you *know* he's prolly at a casino. Sittin around some Caribbean Stud table, whishin he had enough money for the V.I.P room.

MARYANNE. Sandy Baranowski saw him at the Harrah's in Joliet and she said he mostly plays Roulette now. Roulette and Let it Ride.

DENNIS. Loser.

MARYANNE. Don't talk that way about your father. Even if he made some mistakes, he's still your father.

(A pause. He puts his pants back on. She sits next to him on the bed.)

MARYANNE. Dennis, at home when we listened to the CD you said you liked the play.

DENNIS. I was lyin.

MARYANNE. I sat with you at the kitchen table and you started tappin your foot and you got goosebumps on your arm.

DENNIS. I got goosebumps cause I was so embarrassed for you.

MARYANNE. Oh you were not. You got legitimate Hollywood chills and your eyes did that thing they do when you're emotional. Especially when the young couple started singin that song about the snow and how the ingénue wanted to cover her loverboy with that homemade blanket of cigarette cartons and dishrags. And when the homosexual electronics genius and the Latino drag queen do the kung fu love rap you laughed your head off.

DENNIS. I did not.

MARYANNE. You did too, Dennis. We both laughed our heads off, actually, cause it was funny.

DENNIS. Cause it was stupid.

MARYANNE. It was funny. In fact, you were the first one who laughed – Aunt Billy as my witness. It was genuinely comedic and you know it...Dennis?

DENNIS. What.

MARYANNE. We don't know how much time I got left, you know?

DENNIS. Don't be so fuckin morbid.

(She slaps him hard. He rises, crosses to the window, holding his face.)

MARYANNE. Oh, honey, I didn't mean to do that.

DENNIS. Yeah, right.

(She rises, crosses to him.)

MARYANNE. I didn't, I really didn't.

DENNIS. *(turning to her)* Sometimes I wish you would just die and get it over with.

(She moves to touch him. He leans away, crosses to the closet, enters, closing the closet behind him.)

MARYANNE. I realize you're angry. I'm sorry. Dennis…

(no response)

MARYANNE. Dennis, please…

(no response)

MARYANNE. I wish we could be kinder to each other, you know? Figure out some way to…I realize this hasn't been easy on you. You've been so brave.

DENNIS. *(from inside the closet)* Just take your new lover to the play, okay?

MARYANNE. He's not my new lover.

DENNIS. *(from inside the closet)* Whatever.

MARYANNE. You should come down and say hello. Just to make sure he doesn't have an axe under his dashboard. Or any suspicious-lookin suitcases floatin around.

DENNIS. *(from inside the closet)* No thanks.

MARYANNE. Well, don't say I didn't try. I guess you can just stay in the closet and not experience life!

(She quickly crosses to the bathroom, closes the door. The sound of the radio. Moments later we hear her vomiting.)

*(**DENNIS** enters from the closet, quickly crosses to the chair, removes the jacket from under the cushion, quickly mashes the inside of the jacket together, squeezes it into a ball and arranges in the corner by the table.)*

*(A sharp cry of pain form the bathroom, then only the radio. **DENNIS** slowly crosses to the bathroom door, puts his hand on it.)*

DENNIS. Ma, you okay?…Ma?

(The radio is turned off. She opens the bathroom door.)

MARYANNE. Will you get me my cane?

(He gets her cane, hands it to her.)

DENNIS. Maybe you should stay in.

MARYANNE. No, I'm gonna go. *(spotting her jacket)* There it is.

(She crosses to the jacket, bends down for it, can't quite reach it. DENNIS moves to help her.)

MARYANNE. I got it.

(She manages to get it, puts it on, crosses to her purse, takes out a twenty, offers it.)

MARYANNE. In case you want a Starbucks or somethin.

(DENNIS takes it, keeps looking at her.)

MARYANNE. What.

DENNIS. Your lipstick.

MARYANNE. What wrong with it? Is it too much?

DENNIS. You look like a corpse.

(She dabs her lips with a tissue.)

MARYANNE. Is that better?

(DENNIS nods.)

MARYANNE. So I guess I'll see you later, then. Gimme a hug, huh?

(He hugs her. She crosses to the front door. DENNIS moves to open it for her. She exits. After the door closes, DENNIS, drops to his knees, cries for a moment, slaps himself in the face, punches himself in the legs, gets himself together, crosses to the bedside table, takes her bottle of pain medication, removes the top, takes a pill, then exits the room, leaving the door open. He returns moments later with a bucket of ice, exits again, leaving the door open. A young woman enters, looks around, a little on edge. She is well dressed, haute couture, heels. DENNIS' cell phone rings a few times. She spots it, picks it up, doesn't answer, sets it down just as DENNIS enters with three cans of Coke Classic.)

FRANCES. Hey.

DENNIS. Hey.

FRANCES. Is that your cell phone?

DENNIS. Yeah.

FRANCES. It was just ringing.

(He does not cross to it.)

FRANCES. I just saw you down by the ice machine. I waved hello, did you see me?

DENNIS. No.

FRANCES. I thought that boy's either rude or he's blind.

DENNIS. I'm not blind.

FRANCES. Full-blown wave.

(He checks the bathroom, the closet.)

FRANCES. I normally wouldn't just invite myself in.

DENNIS. But you did.

FRANCES. Well, you seemed like a nice guy. From a distance at least. In your Run DMC sweats and Supersize hoody. Are you a nice guy?

DENNIS. Who are you?

FRANCES. Just a girl who's all dressed up with nowhere to go. Can I ask you a question?

(He doesn't answer.)

FRANCES. Well I will anyway. What's a kid like you doing holed up in New York City hotel room on a Saturday night?

DENNIS. Who said I was holed up?

FRANCES. Oh, so he *chooses* solitude. So independent.

DENNIS. What are you doin in my room?

FRANCES. That's a good question. I was just...I don't know. I actually have no idea why I'm in your room. I walked in. Sometimes life is like a river and you have to do all you can to avoid the piranhas, right? But while we're on the subject, would you mind if I hung out with you for a little while? I'm harmless, I promise. And speaking of rivers I'm a swimming conversationalist, I really am.

DENNIS. What do you mean, a kid like me?

FRANCES. I don't follow.

DENNIS. Before you asked why a kid like me's –

FRANCES. I guess you just don't seem like a shut-in.

DENNIS. What do I seem like?

FRANCES. A mover. A shaker. A stuffin of mudliness.

DENNIS. A mud stuffin?

FRANCES. Exactly. What were you doing at the ice machine, anyway?

DENNIS. Getting ice.

FRANCES. For what?

DENNIS. Cooling purposes.

FRANCES. Nice. First time in New York? I only ask because along with your natural virility you possess a skosh of that don't stab me my skin breaks easily look.

DENNIS. *Skosh?*

FRANCES. Let's start over, shall we? Hi, I just saw you in the hall a few minutes ago. You were getting ice out of the ice machine. My name is Frances.

(*She approaches him, extends her hand. He drops a can of Coke, picks it up. They shake.*)

FRANCES. And you're…

DENNIS. Dennis.

FRANCES. You look like a Dennis. A Dennis or a Nick. By the way, Dennis, is there anything to drink around here, besides Coca-Cola Classic?

(**DENNIS** *crosses to his gym bag, pulls out a bottle of whiskey.*)

FRANCES. Jackpot music. Where'd you score that?

DENNIS. This dude down by the front desk hooked me up.

FRANCES. Tall, storkish-looking guy with a long skinny face? Balding? Big fake white teeth?

DENNIS. Yeah.

FRANCES. That's Creepy Chris. He apparently won the teeth at a poker game. He pretends he works at the hotel. He sort of hangs out in the lobby and wears the bellboy uni. Be careful of him, his hands tend to wander.

DENNIS. Whoa.

FRANCES. How old are you, Dennis?

DENNIS. Um, old…I'm seventeen.

FRANCES. Seventeen but you still get fucked up like the rest of America? Sit down I'll make us some drinks.

(She takes the bottle, opens a Coke, puts ice in glasses, makes Jack and Cokes. He sits in the overstuffed chair.)

FRANCES. Who was that woman who left a few minutes ago?

DENNIS. My mom.

FRANCES. Where was she going?

DENNIS. To a play.

FRANCES. Which one?

DENNIS. That famous one where everyone's dyin.

FRANCES. The musical of all musicals? Everyone's dying and falling in love and freezing to death and singing about it?

DENNIS. Survivin.

FRANCES. *Survivin! Call Telecharge, blah blah, blah.* There's a movie now.

DENNIS. Yeah, don't remind me.

FRANCES. She seemed stressed.

DENNIS. *(standing)* Were you like spyin on our room or somethin?

FRANCES. Me? A spy? God, no. What would I be spying on, anyway?

DENNIS. Not much. Boredom. Stupidity.

FRANCES. Siddown, sailor.

(He sits.)

FRANCES. So, it's that bad, huh? Why does she have a cane?

DENNIS. Bad ankle.

(She hands him a drink.)

FRANCES. To boredom and stupidity. Cheers.

DENNIS. Cheers.

(They clink glasses.)

FRANCES. Let's try that again. Look me in the eye this time. Lack of eye contact during a toast brings about bad luck. Cheers.

(He looks her in the eye.)

DENNIS. Cheers.

(They clink glasses again, drink.)

FRANCES. So, what's Mom so stressed about?

DENNIS. She's just pissed cause I wouldn't go to the play with her.

FRANCES. Not a big theatre buff?

DENNIS. Not really.

FRANCES. You ever been to a play?

DENNIS. I saw *A Christmas Carol* in Chicago when I was like four.

FRANCES. Tiny Tim didn't do it for you?

DENNIS. No.

FRANCES. I saw A Christmas Carol at Madison Square Garden a few years ago. This octogenarian from General Hospital was Scrooge. Tiny Tim was played by some Olympic silver medalist figure skater. Katie Chong or Pong or Wakazashi or some shit.

DENNIS. What's an octogenarian?

FRANCES. A person in their eighties. Watch out, they're taking over the world. Or at least a theater near you… So, you've only seen one play?

DENNIS. Uh-huh.

FRANCES. How do you know you don't like theatre?

DENNIS. I just do.

FRANCES. Don't be so provincial.

DENNIS. What?

FRANCES. You're obviously from the Midwest, tell me I'm wrong.

DENNIS. You're not.

FRANCES. What part?

DENNIS. Illinois.

FRANCES. Then you're forgiven. For now at least. There's still hope.

DENNIS. Hope for what?

FRANCES. That you'll turn out okay. A little culture's good for the glands, eh?

DENNIS. You an actress or somethin?

FRANCES. Memorize all those lines? No fucking way.

DENNIS. What do you do?

FRANCES. Go to parties. Ride around in antique sports cars. Eat three hundred dollar meals financed by middle-aged men with silver hair and glucosamine sulfate addictions.

DENNIS. So you're like a hooker?

FRANCES. You wish...I used to work at a Gallery. Now I basically get away with stuff and get to dress up nice for it. How's that for a job description?

DENNIS. Where are you from?

FRANCES. Where do you *think* I'm from?

DENNIS. I don't know. Here.

FRANCES. As in I was born under the candy machine on the fourth floor? What part of Illinois?

DENNIS. Freeport.

FRANCES. Where's that?

DENNIS. Northwest corner of the state. Sorta near Iowa.

FRANCES. Corn.

DENNIS. Yeah.

FRANCES. Corn, cattle, and combines.

DENNIS. Pretty much.

FRANCES. You live on a farm?

DENNIS. No.

FRANCES. Shorn any sheep in your day? Tipped your favorite bovine?

DENNIS. I've de-tasseled corn.

FRANCES. Oooh, rebel rebel.

DENNIS. You prolly don't even know what a combine is.

FRANCES. Sure I do.

DENNIS. What is it?

FRANCES. It's one of those big, bulky tractor-type-things that...combines.

DENNIS. Not really.

FRANCES. Give a city girl a break, huh?

(A knock on the door. She freezes, then gestures that she isn't there and that she is going into the bathroom, quietly exits to the bathroom, shuts the door. He hides the whiskey in the desk drawer, crosses to the front door, opens it. He speaks to someone, closes the door, returns with a small white bag.)

*(**FRANCES** reenters, holding cassette tapes.)*

FRANCES. Who was it?

DENNIS. Some creature from the front desk.

FRANCES. The redhead or the Puerto Rican?

DENNIS. Maybe the redhead.

FRANCES. Six-six? Rockabilly fauxhawk.

(He nods.)

FRANCES. What'd he want?

(He holds up the bag, then reaches into it, removes a small stuffed bear wearing an "I Heart NYC" T-shirt.)

FRANCES. Cute. Secret admirer?

DENNIS. I wish. It's from my mom. She can't resist the gift shop. She's like one of those fat ladies at the mall. If she gets a whiff of the caramel corn she can't stop shoppin. Yesterday she went down for Starbucks and came back with a Statue of Liberty paperweight and three souvenir spoons. *(He grabs the stuffed monkey.)* And this guy traveled with us all the way from Illinois. He's her spiritual advisor.

(He throws the monkey on the floor and it screeches a few times. The joke doesn't go over well. He banishes the monkey to the drawer of the armoire.)

FRANCES. Is the bear for you?

DENNIS. It's prolly for my Aunt Billy.

FRANCES. You have an aunt named Billy?

DENNIS. Her real name is Diana but everyone calls her Billy – don't ask me why. She sorta looks like John Goodman from *The Big Lebowski.*

FRANCES. Yikes...*(holding the cassette tapes up)* Cassettes from the bathroom: The Bangles, Juice Newton, and... Maryanne's Magical Mystery Mix?

DENNIS. They're my mom's.

FRANCES. Festive.

(She sets the cassettes on the table, returns to making her drink, can't find the whiskey.)

DENNIS. It's in the drawer.

(She opens the drawer, retrieves the whiskey, makes her drink.)

FRANCES. So what's with all the medical stuff in the bathroom?

DENNIS. It's for my mom.

FRANCES. When I saw her in the hallway didn't seem *that* old. Aside from the cane I spose.

DENNIS. She's forty-seven.

FRANCES. What's her deal?

DENNIS. She just has a hard time standin for too long.

FRANCES. She's got some sort of condition?

DENNIS. You could say that.

FRANCES. Like arthritis?

DENNIS. That's part of it. So are you all dressed up cause some old guy's waitin for you?

FRANCES. I was supposed to go to this thing over at Tavern on the Green. But I changed my mind so now I'm here. With you. Don't worry, Dennis, your mom won't mind.

DENNIS. I didn't say she would.

FRANCES. You guys make a cute couple. I saw you earlier. Down in the lobby. She was holding onto your arm. You're quite the gentleman.

(FRANCES' cell phone makes a sound. She looks at it, a bit tense.)

FRANCES. Did you know that Elizabeth Taylor owns a Van Gogh that was looted by the Nazis? That's some crazy shit, huh?

DENNIS. I guess.

(She downs her drink in one gulp.)

FRANCES. So how long are you and your mom in New York?

DENNIS. Just through the weekend.

FRANCES. Aren't you in school?

DENNIS. I'm on spring break.

FRANCES. Shouldn't you be down in Florida doing the Girls Gone Wild thing?

DENNIS. I wish.

FRANCES. I can't imagine spring break with mom being too thrilling.

DENNIS. Lately I've been gettin this creepy feelin she thinks we're datin.

FRANCES. That's so Greek.

DENNIS. Greeks date their children?

FRANCES. They date em. Fuck em. Cook em in stews...So Mom gets on your nerves, huh? Clingy?

DENNIS. That's an understatement.

FRANCES. She still tucks you in at night? Stirs your Ovaltine, sudsies your hair in the bathtub?

DENNIS. She's just annoying.

FRANCES. You ever fantasize about offing her?

(DENNIS *says nothing.*)

FRANCES. It's okay, Dennis, it's totally normal. When I was in high school I used to sit in class after class and draw pictures of how I would kill my mom. Elaborate pencil sketches that would take hours. Hangings. Public stonings. Boiling water. Birds attacking her. A saw.

DENNIS. What'd you do with the drawings?

FRANCES. After she kicked me out of the house I started mailing them to her once a week. That lasted for about a year.

DENNIS. What'd you get kicked out of the house for?

FRANCES. Partying. Bringing guys home. Fucking my shrink in her four-poster bed. Catholics can't handle anything...Don't say you've never thought about it.

DENNIS. What, being Catholic?

(*His cell phone rings. He looks at it.*)

FRANCES. Who is it?

DENNIS. Um, my dad.

FRANCES. Aren't you gonna answer it?

(*He answers it, crosses to the bathroom, enters the bathroom. During the phone call,* FRANCES *looks at the framed photos on the bedsides stand. She also sees the pain medication.*)

DENNIS. Hello?...Hey...Nothin. Watchin basketball...The Knicks... No...She went to that play...No...Cause I didn't wanna...I don't know...Okay...Yeah, she's *fine*... Where are you?...Why?...What's that in the background?...Dad, don't *(He almost loses it.)* Come on, Dad.

(*He reenters.* FRANCES *quickly sets a picture back on the bedside stand.*)

FRANCES. Everything okay?

DENNIS. Everything's fine.

FRANCES. What's up with him?

DENNIS. I can't really talk about it.

FRANCES. Is he some sort of criminal?

DENNIS. I wish.

FRANCES. Where is he?

DENNIS. He won't say.

FRANCES. Mysterious. What does he do?

DENNIS. He's a professional coward.

FRANCES. Tough times for Dennis.

    (He grabs the cassettes off the table, returns them to the bathroom.)

FRANCES. At least admit that you've thought about it... You've seen it go down in your head. A safe lands on her. She gets sucked into the sky by a tornado. She falls into a bottomless pit.

DENNIS. *(reentering)* A pillow.

FRANCES. A pillow. Peaceful.

DENNIS. Why peaceful?

FRANCES. Middle of the night. The moon silvering the window. The sound of a train in the distance. What do you do?

DENNIS. I stand over her bed while she's sleepin...

FRANCES. And then...

DENNIS. And then I press it into her face until she stops...

FRANCES. Stops what?

DENNIS. Breathin.

FRANCES. Well, that's awfully gentle. You realize you'll have to break her neck, too, right?

DENNIS. Why?

FRANCES. Because you have to make sure. You'd hate her to suddenly come up for air. This is the kind of thing you definitely want finality with.

DENNIS. I've thought about a hammer, too. I sneak up behind her when she's doin the dishes.

FRANCES. And...

DENNIS. She's hummin to the radio.

FRANCES. Easy listening?

DENNIS. Classic Eighties.

FRANCES. The Bangles?

DENNIS. Lionel Richie.

FRANCES. Dancin on the ceiling. Then what?

DENNIS. After the first one she goes to a knee. Like she's tyin her shoelace. Then I keep hittin her till her brains spill out.

FRANCES. *(producing a cell phone)* Do me a favor, call this number and hit pound.

(DENNIS starts to take her phone, hesitates.)

DENNIS. Who am I callin?

FRANCES. Don't worry it's nobody important.

DENNIS. Why can't you?

FRANCES. Superstition.

(He takes her cell phone.)

FRANCES. You got nice eyes, by the way, Dennis. Warm.

(He makes the call, waits. She turns away. After a moment, he hits pound, offers the phone. She remains turned away.)

DENNIS. Don't you want your phone back?

(She reaches back for it. He crosses to her, places it in her hand.)

DENNIS. What did I just do?

(She sits. She cries.)

DENNIS. Did I just do somethin?

(She continues crying. He crosses to the box of tissues, crosses back, hands it to her.)

FRANCES. Hey, can I borrow twenty bucks?

(He reaches into his pocket, hands her the twenty bucks that MARYANNE had given him.)

DENNIS. You don't have to pay me back.

(*She wads the Kleenex.*)

FRANCES. So tell me about your school.

DENNIS. It's a military academy.

FRANCES. Boarding?

DENNIS. Yep.

FRANCES. Does it suck as much as I think it does?

DENNIS. Prolly more.

FRANCES. Where is it?

DENNIS. Wisconsin.

FRANCES. Scary place.

DENNIS. You been there?

FRANCES. I was in Milwaukee for a few days once. Smelled like shit. Everyone kept saying it was from a chocolate factory but it reeked of sewage to me. Lots of fat people. Fudruckers and Tanning salons.

DENNIS. My school's in Delafield. It's like twenty minutes north of Milwaukee.

FRANCES. So you know. Why'd you get shipped off – you a fuckup or something?

DENNIS. I don't know.

FRANCES. Oh, come on, Dennis. Military school?

DENNIS. I guess my parents think I don't care about anything.

FRANCES. They send you to military school for apathy? Most people go to shrinks for that.

DENNIS. They tried that for a while, too, but it didn't work.

FRANCES. So you're a genuine lost cause.

DENNIS. I guess.

FRANCES. So is it true?

DENNIS. What.

FRANCES. That you don't care about anything?

DENNIS. I care about shit.

FRANCES. Like what?

DENNIS. I don't know. Basketball.

FRANCES. Basketball doesn't count. That's a hobby.

DENNIS. It's actually a sport.

FRANCES. Are you like going pro or something?

DENNIS. No. But I'm on the varsity.

FRANCES. Ooh, he's on the varsity. Do the cheerleaders bake brownies and ruffle their pompoms for you?

DENNIS. We don't have cheerleaders. We have these roided out guys who wear turtlenecks and paint their faces red. They're called rabble-rousers. When the other team shoots free throws they always rip their shirts off and start flexing.

FRANCES. Sexy.

DENNIS. It's pretty embarrassing.

FRANCES. So aside from basketball, don't you have any big dreams?

DENNIS. No.

FRANCES. What do you want to be when you grow up?

DENNIS. I don't know. Nothing.

FRANCES. Come on, really? When you were a little boy didn't you fantasize about being a firefighter? Or a cowboy?

DENNIS. A *cowboy*?

FRANCES. What about a policeman? Cops are hot.

DENNIS. We have this little man in our front yard. Like next to the mailbox. He has a beard and a pointy hat. He's ceramic or clay or whatever. I used to fantasize that I could somehow crack the thing open and step inside and close it around me and become him. Like my arms would become his arms and my face would become his face.

FRANCES. And then what – you head to the Javitz Center?

DENNIS. What? No. I'd just stand there.

FRANCES. Next to the mailbox.

DENNIS. Yeah.

FRANCES. Keeping sentry over the greater good of man for fifty-odd years.

DENNIS. Or long enough until someone bashes my head in with a baseball bat.

FRANCES. You want to grow up to be a lawn gnome.

DENNIS. I guess.

FRANCES. And then have your head bashed in.

DENNIS. We have a fake deer, too.

FRANCES. So our man's into ceramics. There's a start.

DENNIS. What about you? What do you want to be?

(Her phone makes a noise. He grabs it, starts to hand it to her.)

FRANCES. What does it say?

DENNIS. It says, "Have A Good Trip."

FRANCES. Hey, you mind if I smoke in here?

DENNIS. It's a No Smoking room.

FRANCES. Yeah, but they don't care. I see the cleaning ladies smoking all the time. Changing the beds, smoking their Newports. Watching Oprah.

(She takes out a pack of expensive cigarettes, crosses to the fire alarm over the table, dismantles it, removes the nine-volt.)

FRANCES. Want one?

DENNIS. No thanks.

FRANCES. Wise of you to steer clear. Expensive habit.

(She produces a cigarette, lights it, smokes, standing on the table, playfully walking around it.)

FRANCES. So military school. That's like yes sir and no sir and all that, right?

DENNIS. Pretty much.

FRANCES. What's your school called?

DENNIS. Buckner.

FRANCES. Buckner. Sounds like the name of a horse. A big brown horse with a limp. You going into the Army after you graduate?

DENNIS. No way. I fuckin hate the military.

FRANCES. Is your dad a general or something?

DENNIS. No.

FRANCES. He's too busy cornering the coward market?

DENNIS. He used to work for Metlife but now he mostly gambles. Last year he secretly mortgaged our house and lost close to fifty grand.

FRANCES. Your parents still together?

DENNIS. They're separated.

(She steps down from the table.)

FRANCES. So are there any chicks hanging around that school?

DENNIS. Townies mostly.

FRANCES. Fat girls with beards?

DENNIS. What?

FRANCES. Townies. That's what the word brings to mind. I see Paul Bunyan in a gingham dress.

DENNIS. Some of them are actually pretty hot.

FRANCES. Oh yeah? Like who?

DENNIS. Like this girl you wouldn't know.

FRANCES. What's her name?

DENNIS. Kim.

FRANCES. She fine, huh?

DENNIS. Yeah.

FRANCES. You've gotten to second base with her yet? Boobies?

DENNIS. Maybe.

FRANCES. Send her dirty emails?

DENNIS. We email.

FRANCES. Cybersex is hot.

DENNIS. It's not cybersex.

FRANCES. Dear Townie Kim. I can't stop thinking about your vigorous beard. Soon I'll be able to grow one too and we'll grapple and make woodcuts. Yours Truly, Cadet Dennis...So is Townie Kim your sweetheart, your lady, your around-the-way girl?

DENNIS. Not really.

FRANCES. Why not?

DENNIS. I don't know. Ask her.

FRANCES. You're fresh-faced and hot in a sort of boy-scout-Meets-Luke-Skywalker kind of way. Are you gay?

DENNIS. What? No. Why, do I seem gay?

FRANCES. Not really, but these days you never know, right? *(studying him)* You'd probably look really good with long hair. It looks good short, too, but I'll bet it would be nice long.

(He starts laughing, almost falls.)

FRANCES. What?

DENNIS. I feel like spaghetti.

FRANCES. You hungry? We could order room service.

DENNIS. No, I took one of my mom's Vicodins. *(He starts making wavy motions with his arms.)* I feel like spaghetti.

(She laughs, slips into the bathroom. "White Rabbit" starts to play and then **FRANCES** *reenters with a small boombox with a cassette player. She lip syncs to "White Rabbit," dances toward* **DENNIS** *theatrically.* **DENNIS** *attempts to play along for a while, but stops suddenly, crosses to the boombox, stops it.*)*

DENNIS. Are we like falling in love?

FRANCES. I don't know. Are we?

(He takes a step toward her, starts to raise his hand to her face.)

FRANCES. *(killing the attempt)* Hey, would you mind if I took a nap? I haven't slept in a few days. I'm pretty beat.

DENNIS. Go head.

*See Music Use Note on Page 3

(She crosses to the beds.)

FRANCES. Which one's yours?

DENNIS. That one.

(She removes her heels, pulls the covers back, gets in bed.)

FRANCES. Come sit.

(He crosses to the bed, sits. After a short silence:)

FRANCES. Hey, know any songs?

DENNIS. Like what?

FRANCES. I don't know. Anything. Know any Simon and Garfunkel?

DENNIS. No.

FRANCES. You don't know any Simon and Garfunkel? You really are young. You a virgin?

DENNIS. Negative.

FRANCES. Come on. Military school. Townie Kim. It's not your fault, Dennis. Don't worry, it'll eventually happen. Anyway, losing it's not as great or as terrible as you'd imagine. It's sort of like cocaine.

DENNIS. I went AWOL a few weeks ago. Met her on this hiking trail.

FRANCES. And?

DENNIS. And we started messin around, but –

FRANCES. You forgot the condom.

DENNIS. No.

FRANCES. She had a migraine.

DENNIS. No.

FRANCES. You discovered you had an unexpected leaky rash.

DENNIS. No.

FRANCES. You're so huge you couldn't get it out of your fatigue trousers.

DENNIS. What?

FRANCES. I'm kidding. What happened?

DENNIS. I just...I don't know.

FRANCES. Hey, getting it up on a hiking trail isn't easy. It was probably cold out.

DENNIS. It was like thirty-five degrees.

FRANCES. See? So now you send dirty emails to each other. All isn't lost. Townie Kim's probably waiting for you to come back with bated breath.

DENNIS. I don't wanna go back. I hate that fuckin school.

FRANCES. What about the basketball team?

DENNIS. I'm seventh man. I only play half the game if I'm lucky, and the coach doesn't let me shoot unless I have an uncontested layup...I keep thinkin about leavin the hotel, like goin through the front doors and turnin left and just walkin till I disappear into some other building or life or whatever.

FRANCES. You should head down to the South Street Seaport. Get on the Staten Island Ferry. Getting on a boat can change your life. The water. Seagulls. Manhattan receding in the distance. The buildings shrinking like toys...*(drifting off)* Simon and Garfunkle have this song about the seasons. Leaves changing. Memories. Bitter sweet farewells. It's such a pretty one...*(drifting further yet)*...Will you put your hand on my head?

(He hesitates, but does so.)

FRANCES. Pat it.

(He does.)

FRANCES. That's it...Dennis, that thing with your mom and the hammer. It's just a hammer. And she's just a mom. It's like anything else, you know?

(She sings softly for a moment and then falls asleep. He watches her as lights fade.)

End of Act I

ACT II

(DENNIS is asleep in the overstuffed chair, curled up. The bed is neatly made and FRANCES is gone. The teddy bear is on top of the pillows. On the nightstand, standing upright, is a hammer. It's a simple twelve-inch hammer with a wooden handle. The hotel room phone rings. DENNIS wakes, crosses to the phone, answers it.)

DENNIS. Hello?...Hello?...Ma?

(He hangs up, takes the hammer in his hand, considers it, sets it down. He crosses to the bathroom, enters, runs the sink. FRANCES enters with a key card. She is no longer wearing the dress, a small gym bag on her shoulder. She now wears something simple, jeans and a sweater, sneakers. Her hair is also different and she's no longer wearing makeup. She crosses to the table, grabs tissues, and wipes down her cell phone, quietly places it next to the room phone. Just as she is dropping the tissue in the wastebasket, DENNIS enters from the bathroom.)

FRANCES. Hey.

DENNIS. Hey. Did you just call?

FRANCES. No.

DENNIS. You changed.

FRANCES. I'd rather not travel in Yves Saint Laurent. Besides, it's getting cold out. The temperature must have dropped fifteen degrees. You were dead asleep when I left. You talk, you know?

DENNIS. What was I sayin?

FRANCES. It was utterly unintelligible, but it had a rhythm. For a second I thought you were rapping.

DENNIS. What's in the bag?

FRANCES. Basically my entire life.

DENNIS. Where you goin?

FRANCES. North.

DENNIS. As in the North Pole?

FRANCES. Yeah, I'm gonna start my life over as one of Santa's elves. We'll run into each other in twenty years and you'll be a gnome and I'll be an elf.

DENNIS. Okay. *(pointing to the hammer)* Where'd that come from?

FRANCES. What, that twelve-inch Black and Decker hammer? I have my connections.

(beat)

FRANCES. So Dennis I need you to promise me something, okay?

DENNIS. What.

FRANCES. If anyone comes around asking whether you saw me tonight say no.

DENNIS. Who would come around asking that?

FRANCES. Nobody you would know.

DENNIS. Are you like in a James Bond movie or somethin?

FRANCES. Just promise me.

DENNIS. Why should I?

FRANCES. Look, Dennis, this is what's going on: For the past ten months I've been seeing a man. A very wealthy, very powerful, very charming, very well known *married* man who owns a fortune five hundred company and who is old enough to be my father. About three months after we started seeing each other I got pregnant from this man. And shortly thereafter, he asked me to get an abortion. I wanted to keep the baby. He didn't. He already had four children – all adults now – and he wanted no part of that. He offered me a lot of money. And ultimately a deal was struck to the tune of a hundred thousand dollars. Money I was to be paid immediately following the procedure. We went to a very exclusive, private clinic. Things were really hard for me after that. And when I say hard I mean hard to be alive. Hard to see his face. Hard to be reminded of the loss. Hard to not feel like I was floating around in someone else's life. But somehow the most difficult thing of all was the realization that the money was never going to come.

FRANCES. *(cont.)* Since I've been feeling better, we've been meeting here in the city, where he rents me an apartment in Chelsea. But to keep things neat, we rarely stay there. In fact, we mostly tuck ourselves away in places like this and he pays cash and uses an alias, covers all his tracks. But the more we meet the more the subject of the money seems to fade.

So this weekend I made a special arrangement of my own, because you see one can only feel like a fool for so long. And about an hour ago, after he unwittingly swallowed a powerful sleeping pill and passed out, he was photographed by a major tabloid photographer, for which I was handsomely paid. So he's currently lying facedown in his birthday suit in a room on the floor below this one, almost directly under the ice machine. And soon I will take the elevator down to the lobby, get in a taxi, and leave this miserable fucking city, forgetting our rendezvous at various midlevel Midtown hotels. The vacation to London where he told me he loved me on Waterloo Bridge. The black market Viagra dealers we've gotten to know. How he needed me to bury my finger halfway up his ass so he could come. The night we spent in Mount Sinai's emergency room because he thought he was having a heart attack. The dresses he bought me. The pearls and the earrings and the three-thousand-dollar shoes from Bergdorf's. The restaurants and his fucking cronies who would all but grope my ass when he was in the bathroom pissing out multiple martinis.

You see, Dennis, he had a chance. I decided that tonight was his final opportunity to make good on the money. But before he got in the shower, just a few minutes after our last fuck, I asked him about it and

FRANCES. *(cont.)* he said that it wasn't going to happen. He called me stupid and told me I was lucky to still be in his life.

So earlier when you called that number and hit pound you set it all in motion, Dennis. You cued the photographer to make his way up from the lobby. And after you fell asleep, I went down to the fifteenth floor and met him and undressed and crawled under my ex-lover's body and made erotic fuck me faces and fondled his flaccid penis and positioned his face just right for the camera. Hell, I even strapped one on and got a little kinky. And when it was over I gathered my things and said goodbye to his body. Which looks somehow smaller while he sleeps. Feeble even.

(a pause)

FRANCES. I tell you all of this because I feel I can trust you.

DENNIS. Can I ask you a question?

FRANCES. Of course.

DENNIS. If they paid you handsomely for those photographs, why did you have to borrow twenty bucks from me?

FRANCES. Because they cut me a check. I happen to be cash poor at the moment...Do you need me to show it to you?

DENNIS. And if this is all true, then why did you come back here?

FRANCES. Because I wanted to thank you for helping me out. So thank you.

DENNIS. Sure.

FRANCES. And I wanted to say good-by.

DENNIS. Are you still in love with him?

*(The door opens. **MARYANNE** enters with **HERMAN**, African-American, mid fifties. They are in high spirits, mid-conversation when **MARYANNE** sees **FRANCES**, stops.)*

FRANCES. Hi.

MARYANNE. Hi.

DENNIS. Did you just call?

MARYANNE. Me? No. Why, did someone call?

FRANCES. I'm Frances.

(She approaches **MARYANNE,** *hand extended.)*

MARYANNE. Maryanne Bales.

FRANCES. Pleased to meet you.

(They shake.)

MARYANNE. Do we know you?

DENNIS. I met her in the hall.

FRANCES. We met by the ice machine.

DENNIS. I was gettin ice.

MARYANNE. Ice for what?

FRANCES. Cooling purposes.

DENNIS. My ankle. I turned it.

MARYANNE. Are you okay?

DENNIS. I'm fine. It was nothin. It's not even swollen.

MARYANNE. Who called?

DENNIS. There was no one on the other end.

MARYANNE. Your cell?

DENNIS. The room phone.

(awkward pause)

HERMAN. I'm Herman. You must be Dennis.

*(***HERMAN*** approaches* **DENNIS,** *his hand outstretched. They shake.)*

HERMAN. Pleased to meet you.

DENNIS. Nice to meet you.

HERMAN. Thanks for the ticket, by the way.

DENNIS. Sure.

FRANCES. *(to* **HERMAN***)* I'm Frances.

HERMAN. Nice to meet you, Frances.

(**HERMAN** *and* **FRANCES** *shake.*)

FRANCES. Nice to meet you.

(*Awkward pause. All are frozen, looking at each other.*)

FRANCES. So how was the play? Dennis told me you went to see the famous musical.

MARYANNE. The play was good. In fact, I would even say it was great, right Herman?

HERMAN. I liked it very much. Powerful, powerful stuff.

MARYANNE. The singin. The dancin. The costumes.

HERMAN. Man, those kids could sing.

MARYANNE. *(to* **DENNIS***)* I bought a T-shirt for Aunt Billie. They didn't have a double-X-L, but the X-L looks pretty big. Some lady said they make em big for the tourists. Not sure what she meant by that exactly.

DENNIS. She prolly meant that tourists are fat.

MARYANNE. Is that true? *(to* **HERMAN***)* Are tourists generally fat?

HERMAN. As far as I know a tourist is a tourist. Same as anybody else.

MARYANNE. *We're* certainly not fat.

DENNIS. Ma, Aunt Billie weighs like three hondo.

MARYANNE. But Aunt Billie isn't a tourist, Dennis. She's barely even left Illinois. You have to *go* places to qualify to be a tourist.

FRANCES. Wouldn't that make us all tourists in some respect?

(*She and* **DENNIS** *share a private look that somehow harkens back to the "White Rabbit" dance.*)

MARYANNE. So what have you two been up to?

DENNIS. Nothin much.

FRANCES. Just hangin out.

DENNIS. Yeah, we're just hangin out.

FRANCES. Shootin the breeze. Passin the time.

MARYANNE. Did the Knicks wind up winnin?

FRANCES. They won by fifteen. Harrington had a great fourth quarter. Finally started putting the ball in the basket.

HERMAN. Then I'm sure they're plenty happy at the Garden. When they win people splurge and take taxis. When they lose they mostly take the subway.

(MARYANNE notices the hammer.)

MARYANNE. What the heck is that?

DENNIS. Um, a hammer.

MARYANNE. What's it doin in here?

FRANCES. When we were watching the game that picture fell off the wall. They sent someone up to fix it and he left the hammer.

MARYANNE. Oh, well I'm glad they fixed it.

FRANCES. Yeah, I find the service to be excellent here.

MARYANNE. Do you?

FRANCES. Yes, I do, actually.

MARYANNE. You find it to be excellent. I'm glad you approve.

(another awkward pause)

HERMAN. Hey, does anybody want any Chinese food? I was thinkin about goin out for some. There's a great place just around the corner.

FRANCES. I'd love some Chinese food, Herman. Egg drop soup. General Tso's cicken.

HERMAN. There you go. Maryanne?

MARYANNE. I guess I could go for some mooshoo pork... Herman, thank you.

HERMAN. Dennis?

DENNIS. Well...Herman, maybe I'll have a hamburger.

MARYANNE. From a friggin Chinese restaurant?

FRANCES. Get the chicken broccoli. Everyone loves chicken broccoli.

MARYANNE. He doesn't like broccoli.

FRANCES. Snow peas, then.

HERMAN. I'd be happy to pop in somewhere else and get you a hamburger, Dennis.

DENNIS. I'll try the chicken broccoli.

HERMAN. Chicken broccoli it is then.

MARYANNE. Maybe we should write all that down for you.

HERMAN. I'll remember it.

(**MARYANNE** *goes for her purse.*)

HERMAN. Oh, no. This one's on me, Maryanne.

MARYANNE. Herman.

HERMAN. After you gave me a ticket to that fantastic play? It's the least I can do. You just sit tight. I'll be right back.

(**HERMAN** *exits.*)

DENNIS. Wow.

MARYANNE. Wow what?

DENNIS. Herman.

MARYANNE. What about him?

DENNIS. *What about him?*

MARYANNE. Yeah, what's the problem?

DENNIS. Nothin, I guess.

MARYANNE. You got an issue with the color of his skin?

DENNIS. Me? I don't care that he's black.

MARYANNE. So what are you sayin exactly?

DENNIS. I'm not sayin nothin. I just wonder what Uncle Stags would think. Or diggity-diggity dad.

MARYANNE. Well, they're not here and it's none of their diggity-diggity dang business.

DENNIS. *(to* **FRANCES**) During Christmas break this black guy stopped at our house and asked for directions to Dubuque and they practically lynched him.

MARYANNE. Oh, they did not either.

DENNIS. Yes they did, Ma. Uncle Stags was about to call the cops on his cell phone. And later that night Dad said he was about thirty seconds from goin and gettin his goddang taser gun from the basement. All the poor guy wanted was directions. Little black guy with a limp.

MARYANNE. Little black guy with a limp, my foot.

DENNIS. It wasn't like he was some gang-banger from Chicago.

MARYANNE. Well, that guy wasn't exactly what you would call a model citizen, either, Dennis. His face was so sweaty and his hands were all fidgety and he didn't smell like roses either.

DENNIS. What did he smell like?

MARYANNE. Well, let's talk a little turkey and at least admit that he smelled *unshowered*, Dennis. Unshowered and like I said he was all sweaty and fidgety. His mouth kept twitchin. I thought he was a goddang crack addict – I'm just bein honest. He had many of the classic signs. The characteristics and whatnot. Your Uncle Stags was just being careful, as was your father. There's nothin wrong with them lookin out for our safety during a suspicious situation like that.

DENNIS. Situation? What situation?

MARYANNE. That guy made you nervous too, Dennis.

DENNIS. I wasn't nervous at all! I'm the one who told him how to get back on Highway Twenty. I thought he was nice. So he twitched a little. He was prolly crazy nervous cause he was in *whiteyville*. Uncle Stags is a racist and that's all I'm sayin. And dad's not exactly what I would call a passionate civil rights activist.

MARYANNE. Your father doesn't have a racist bone in his body.

DENNIS. Not one that he would admit to. During Thanksgiving break we were watchin a Bulls game and he called Derek Rose a happy-go-lucky chuck-it-up brother.

MARYANNE. What's racist about that? Brother's not racist.

DENNIS. *Happy-go-lucky chuck-it-up brother's* not racist? He might as well have called him a porch monkey.

MARYANNE. Brother's not racist, Dennis. Not in my book.

DENNIS. Maybe twenty years ago it wasn't. You can't call black guys brothers anymore. They're African-Americans.

MARYANNE. And we're Scotch-Irish-Welsh-Americans, but no one calls us that. We're caucasian white people, Dennis. American caucasian white people. For godsakes, they call each other *nigga*. *Nigga* this and *nigga* that. I hear it all the time on those rap CDs you listen to. And for your information, smart guy, one of your father's best friends from college was Black. His name was Torris and he was from Orlando Florida and he had a friggin *jerry curl.* He even stood up at our wedding and he was treated just like anybody else. No one even raised an eyebrow. Your father's a racist and I'm Yankee Doodle Dandy...Where's Magic Monkey!? *(turning to* **DENNIS***)* What'd you do with Magic Monkey?!

DENNIS. It's in the drawer.

*(**MARYANNE** opens the drawer, removes Magic Monkey, seats him on the overstuffed chair, arranges him, then crosses to the window, peers out. **FRANCES** grabs her bag, attempts to leave. **DENNIS** steps in front of her. She stops, sets her bag down.)*

FRANCES. *(to* **MARYANNE***)* Tell us more about the play.

MARYANNE. Well, I can say this much. Little JFK Junior over there missed a masterwork.

FRANCES. I hear it just floors you.

MARYANNE. Well, it just really makes you think, ya know?

DENNIS. *(doubtful)* About what?

MARYANNE. Well, about everything, Dennis. About everything that there is, really. Life. Why we're here. What's the point of it all. It really makes you appreciate just bein alive.

And the singin, don't get me started. There's this one song where all the characters come to the edge of the stage and sing a very spiritual song in a thunderous harmony. And when I say thunderous I mean thunderous. Like you could almost expect horses to storm the friggin theater or somethin. Sixteen actors fanned across the entire edge of the stage, singin for their lives. Now if that doesn't move a person I don't know what does.

MARYANNE. *(cont.)* And the lovesick ingénue was really somethin to look at. I don't think I've ever seen prettier red hair. You missed somethin pretty dang special there, Dennis...

FRANCES. Were there a lot of young people in the audience? The reason I ask is because the past few times I went to see a Broadway play, the audience was really old.

DENNIS. Octogenarians.

MARYANNE. Octoga*who?*

DENNIS. Octogenarians. People in their eighties. New vocab word I learned today.

FRANCES. Being in those Broadway audiences was like being trapped in a science fiction novel.

MARYANNE. Well I can assure you there were quite a few young people in this audience. In fact, I would even say it was packed to the gills with the Youth of America. There were old people, too, don't get me wrong. Old people, young people, the middle-aged, all sortsa folks.

FRANCES. Was there a standing ovation at the end?

MARYANNE. There certainly was a standing ovation, yes. I stood and Herman stood and everyone around us was standin and clappin with great fervor. Fervor – how's that for a vocab word, Dennis?

FRANCES. Did you feel the performers deserved it? The last play I went to everyone stood up but I didn't feel like the performers deserved it. And in some ways I think they knew it. You could see it on their faces. The shame.

DENNIS. Hmmm.

FRANCES. It felt to me like the audience was congratulating themselves. For being so brilliant and well dressed and part of a big fancy social club. As if they had all been invited to board an exclusive ocean liner.

MARYANNE. Um, I don't mean to be rude, but who are you exactly?

DENNIS. She's just a friend, Ma.

MARYANNE. A friend from where?

DENNIS. I told you, I met her by the ice machine.

MARYANNE. You met her by the ice machine.

DENNIS. Yes!

FRANCES. I'm just a friend, Maryanne.

MARYANNE. Oh yeah? Define friend.

FRANCES. Pal. Ally. Buddy.

MARYANNE. And where are you from?

FRANCES. I'm originally from St. Louis by way of Santa Fe, New Mexico, but I've been in New York for almost ten years.

MARYANNE. Your family's back in the Midwest?

FRANCES. Some of them are, yes.

MARYANNE. St. Louis, huh?

FRANCES. That's where I grew up, yes. St. Louis and then Santa Fe.

MARYANNE. And where do you live now?

DENNIS. She has an apartment in Chelsea.

MARYANNE. St. Louis is such a beautiful city. Clean. They got that nice old train station. And the Arch. And Busch Stadium of course, but I prefer Wrigley Field bein a Cubs fan and all.

FRANCES. It's been a while since I've been back.

MARYANNE. And what do you do?

FRANCES. As in for a living?

MARYANNE. As in what's your job.

DENNIS. She works at an art gallery.

MARYANNE. Here in the city?

FRANCES. In Chelsea, yes.

DENNIS. Earlier Frances was telling me how...

(Awkward pause. Awkward glances.)

MARYANNE. How what.

FRANCES. Earlier I was telling Dennis how it was recently made public that Elizabeth Taylor owns a Van Gogh painting that was looted by the Nazis. Artworld stuff.

DENNIS. Artworld stuff.

MARYANNE. Artworld stuff, huh?

FRANCES. Yeah. The world of art.

DENNIS. The world of art.

FRANCES. You ever stood before an actual Van Gogh? It's an important part of the culture, Maryanne.

DENNIS. Yeah, Ma, a little culture's good for the glands, eh?

MARYANNE. I'm sorry, but is somethin goin on here that I'm not aware of? Cause I gotta admit this is a pretty strange situation and you're actin awful peculiar, Dennis.

DENNIS. How am I actin peculiar?

MARYANNE. You know dang well you're actin peculiar, bub. You got that look on your face that you get when you're tryin to hide somethin. Have you two been drinkin?

DENNIS. No.

MARYANNE. Lemme smell your breath.

DENNIS. No way. That's weird.

MARYANNE. Dennis MacArthur Bales if you've been drinkin I'm gonna be real upset!

DENNIS. I haven't been drinkin.

MARYANNE. Then why does it smell like alcohol in here?

FRANCES. I had a few drinks earlier tonight, Maryanne.

MARYANNE. Oh yeah? Earlier where? Down at the *ice machine?*

FRANCES. Actually, I was at a bar on the Lower East Side with a few of my colleagues. I had two mixed drinks. They were Jack and Cokes. And I also took a sip of a friend's martini, but I'm twenty-eight years old and I don't think I've done anything wrong.

MARYANNE. Why is a twenty-eight year-old woman hangin out with my sixteen-year-old son?

DENNIS. Seventeen!

MARYANNE. I mean my seventeen-year-old son.

DENNIS. *(to MARYANNE)* Ma, chill, Yo.

MARYANNE. Don't start *Yo*-in me again.

FRANCES. I met your son in the hallway, Maryanne. Just like he told you. It's as simple as that.

MARYANNE. You're a guest of the hotel?

FRANCES. I am, yes.

MARYANNE. What room?

FRANCES. Fifteen twenty-one.

MARYANNE. If you're in fifteen twenty-one, then what the heck are you doin on our floor?

FRANCES. There's no ice machine on the fifteenth floor.

MARYANNE. There isn't.

FRANCES. No. And there's actually a sign directing you to this floor. It says, "For ice, please go to the Sixteenth Floor."

MARYANNE. And if you live in Chelsea, then why are you stayin in this hotel?

FRANCES. *(summoning tears)* It's actually a bit of an embarrassing situation, Maryanne, but my apartment has recently become infested with mice.

DENNIS. She has a mouse problem.

MARYANNE. *(to DENNIS)* Swear to me you haven't been drinkin.

DENNIS. I swear, okay? Why don't you believe me?

MARYANNE. I guess I have no choice, do I? And I wasn't gonna say it but it smells like cigarettes in here, too.

FRANCES. I smoked a cigarette earlier, Maryanne. I didn't realize it was a non-smoking room until your son asked me to put it out. I'm really sorry.

DENNIS. She totally put it out, Ma.

(MARYANNE is suddenly overcome with nausea.)

MARYANNE. Excuse me.

(She exits to the bathroom. The sound of the radio, the sound of vomiting.)

DENNIS. *(loud)* Ma, you okay?

MARYANNE. *(from the bathroom)* I'm fine.

DENNIS. You need me to come in?

MARYANNE. *(from the bathroom, radio off)* No, I'm fine. I just need a minute.

(DENNIS starts for the bathroom. FRANCES stops him, produces a piece of gum from her pocket, shoves it in his mouth, repeats with a second piece. He chews, steps around her and enters the bathroom, closes the door. FRANCES then crosses to MARYANNE's purse, goes through it, removes a small wad of cash, maybe a hundred bucks. DENNIS enters from the bathroom, sees her stealing the money. They share a look. She stuffs the money in her pocket.)

(The sound of MARYANNE turning on the sink, running water. FRANCES crosses to the hammer, crosses to DENNIS, hands it to him just as MARYANNE enters.)

MARYANNE. What are you doin with that?

DENNIS. I was gonna return it.

MARYANNE. Well they're the ones who should come get it. I mean they left it here, right?

FRANCES. Your mother's absolutely right. That's ridiculous.

(FRANCES crosses to the phone, picks it up, presses a number, waits.)

FRANCES. *(into phone)* Yes, earlier this evening a gentleman came to room 1604 to fix a large framed photo that fell off the wall and he left his hammer. Could you please send someone up? Thank you.

(She hangs up.)

MARYANNE. Thank you, Frances.

FRANCES. My pleasure. Are you okay?

MARYANNE. Just a little nauseous.

FRANCES. Is there anything I can do for you?

MARYANNE. No, thanks. Just some fresh air would be nice.

(**MARYANNE** *crosses to the window, opens it, peers out, somehow abstracted.*)

MARYANNE. There's this moment in the play when it starts snowin on stage. The homosexual electronics genius has just died and his Latin boyfriend sings this beautiful song about his lover's hands and how kind they were. When the snow was fallin I kept thinkin that it was snowin outside, too. Like outside the theatre. On the traffic lights and the rooftops. The whole New York City skyline dusted with snow. And when the play was over I was so sure that we would walk outside and it would be snowin these impossibly big flakes and the streets would be all pristine and white. But that's not what happened.

FRANCES. It was actually raining earlier.

MARYANNE. Was it?

FRANCES. Not even a few hours ago.

MARYANNE. But it wasn't snowin?

FRANCES. I'm afraid it wasn't.

MARYANNE. Things never turn out the way you wish they would, do they?

(*a pause*)

FRANCES. Well, I hate leaving a party but I have to catch a train.

DENNIS. What about the Chinese food?

FRANCES. You eat it, Dennis. It turns out I don't have much of an appetite tonight anyway.

MARYANNE. Frances, I'm sorry if I came off as rude before.

FRANCES. It was nothing, Maryanne. You were just doing your job. You're a good mother.

MARYANNE. Thank you.

FRANCES. It was really nice to meet you.

MARYANNE. Nice to meet you, too, Frances.

*(**FRANCES** crosses to **DENNIS**, hugs him. He hugs her back. She whispers something in his ear.)*

FRANCES. Bye.

*(**FRANCES** exits with her bag.)*

MARYANNE. So there's nothin else you need to tell me about that girl?

DENNIS. No.

MARYANNE. Are you sure?

DENNIS. I'm sure.

MARYANNE. Dennis, if you had sex with her –

DENNIS. Ma! I didn't have sex with her! What do you think I am – some sorta gigolo or somethin?

MARYANNE. All I'm sayin is that if you did I just hope you had the good sense to use a friggin condom.

(a knock on the door)

MARYANNE. That must be Herman with the Chinese food. His son's supposedly a heckuva ballplayer, you know. You should ask him about him.

(She turns to the mirror, primps her hair a bit.)

*(**DENNIS** answers the door, speaks to someone, unseen, returns.)*

DENNIS. It was the guy for the hammer…How you feelin?

MARYANNE. Not great, actually. Not great, but I'm hangin in there. Do I look okay?

DENNIS. You look good.

MARYANNE. Really? Do you think I should put some mascara on?

DENNIS. You look nice, Ma.

MARYANNE. I really like this Herman fella. He's such a nice man.

DENNIS. Is he married?

MARYANNE. He was. He and his wife divorced a few years ago. And now she's livin with one of his best friends. Or former best friends, I should say.

DENNIS. That sucks.

MARYANNE. He wants to take me to The Cloisters tomorrow.

DENNIS. What's that?

MARYANNE. It's a museum that overlooks the Hudson River. Apparently it's famous for its tapestries and the whole experience is sposed to be really beautiful. Herman says he goes there to think and that it keeps him humble. Such a positive gentle man.

DENNIS. What about Dad?

MARYANNE. Well, your father's pretty much blown it as far as I'm concerned. He's had his chances.

DENNIS. He called earlier.

MARYANNE. Oh yeah? When?

DENNIS. Right after you left.

MARYANNE. Where was he?

DENNIS. He wouldn't say.

MARYANNE. What'd he want?

DENNIS. I don't know. He kept askin how you were doin.

MARYANNE. What'd you tell him?

DENNIS. I told him you were fine. I think he was at a casino.

MARYANNE. Which one?

DENNIS. I couldn't tell. But I could hear the slot machines in the background.

MARYANNE. Did he ask you to wire him money?

DENNIS. No.

MARYANNE. Dennis…

DENNIS. He didn't, Ma, he really didn't. He started cryin again, though.

MARYANNE. Oh, Jeeze. He's prolly lonely. Maybe I should call him back. *(going for her purse)* Was he on his cell?

DENNIS. Yeah, but don't call him, Ma. Don't feel sorry for him. That's what he wants.

(A knock on the door. MARYANNE sets her purse down. DENNIS answers the door. HERMAN enters with Chinese takeout.)

HERMAN. Chinese food, as promised. Where's Frances?

MARYANNE. She had to catch a train.

HERMAN. Well, that's too bad.

DENNIS. She said we should eat her food.

MARYANNE. Hey, let's drink some champagne. How about that, huh?

(**MARYANNE** *crosses to her bag, removes a bottle of champagne, proceeds to remove the cork.*)

MARYANNE. I got this earlier today. It might be a little warm, but what the heck, right?

HERMAN. Champagne is champagne. No complaints here.

MARYANNE. Dennis, get some of those cups from the bathroom, willya?

(**DENNIS** *exits to the bathroom.*)

HERMAN. Here, let me.

(**HERMAN** *sets the Chinese takeout bag down, takes the magnum of champagne from her, removes the rest of the foil, twists out the cork.* **DENNIS** *enters from the bathroom with three plastic cups in plastic, starts to remove the plastic, passes the cups to* **HERMAN.**)

HERMAN. Veuve Clicquot. Nice.

MARYANNE. Oh, it's nothin, really. Special occasion. New York City. The play. A wonderful night.

(**HERMAN** *pours three cups of champagne, passes one to* **MARYANNE,** *starts to pass* **DENNIS** *his, hesitates.*)

HERMAN. *(to* **DENNIS***)* Can I see some ID?

(**DENNIS** *goes for his wallet.*)

HERMAN. I'm kidding!

(*They all laugh.* **HERMAN** *hands the cup of champagne to* **DENNIS.**)

HERMAN. How bout a toast? To a wonderful night.

MARYANNE. Cheers.

DENNIS. Cheers.

(The all clink glasses and drink.)

HERMAN. Man. I just can't get that play out of my head. That song about findin trash in the East River and building your home out of it. I mean, that's some serious stuff. Survivin, you know

MARYANNE. And the way they brought the big blob of plastic on stage and sang to it. And how that girl with the little arm climbed to the top of it with her rag doll. Dennis, I kid you not it sounded just like the CD. Maybe even better.

HERMAN. Life, you know?

MARYANNE. Life indeed.

DENNIS. Survivin.

HERMAN. *(toasting again)* Survivin!

(They drink.)

MARYANNE. Dennis, Herman's son plays basketball at the University of West Virginia.

HERMAN. *Played.* Brandon was their starting point guard freshman and sophomore year. Led the Big East in steals. But he couldn't keep his grades right. Lost his scholarship. Dropped outta school.

MARYANNE. Oh, well that's too bad.

DENNIS. Where is he now?

HERMAN. To be perfectly honest I couldn't tell you, Dennis. I haven't heard from him since November. Last I knew he was still livin in Morgantown, tryin to get a job. His high school coach was tryin to help place him at Drury University, a Divison Two school out in Springfield, Missouri – had a scholarship lined up and everything – but Brandon didn't want to sit out for a semester. Last time I spoke with his mother she said he was livin with some woman in Pittsburgh. His number kept changin so it's been hard keepin in touch. In December I even drove down to Morgantown and tried to track him down but his coach didn't have any further information. Coach told me he thought Brandon had real promise. Not just as a basketball player but as a person. Hopefully I'll catch up to him soon enough.

MARYANNE. *(offering the swivel chair)* Here, Herman, sit.

HERMAN. Oh, I sit for a livin. Here, you take it.

(She chooses the corner of the bed instead. **HERMAN** *offers his arm, the gentleman. They smile at each other.)*

HERMAN. *(to* **DENNIS***)* Your mother tells me you're quite a ball player yourself.

MARYANNE. He's on the varsity.

HERMAN. You gonna play in college?

DENNIS. I guess. If I go.

MARYANNE. You're goin to college, bub, whether you like it or not.

HERMAN. Sure as hell wish I woulda gone. I wound up joinin the Army.

MARYANNE. Herman served over in Vietnam.

HERMAN. Did a couple of tours toward the end, Seventy-four, Seventy-five. Got lucky, came back in one piece. Met my wife, fell in love, got married, had Brandon, became a cabbie in the greatest city in the world. How's that for a story? Couldn't live anywhere else, really.

DENNIS. How long have you been drivin a taxi?

HERMAN. Believe it or not it'll be twenty years in June. Things have changed quite a bit. Used to be lucky if you could get through a day without gettin held up. Lotta cabbies carried guns, lead pipes, nunchucks. Nowadays they got artist paintings on the hoods, plasma screens in the backseat, credit card swipers. You can practically get a cappuccino made for you.

MARYANNE. Ventay, lotta mocha.

*(***MARYANNE*** *and* ***HERMAN*** *laugh heartily.)*

DENNIS. Did you ever want to do anything else?

HERMAN. When I was a boy I had silly dreams. Mostly I wanted to play third base for the Yankees. After I got back from Vietnam I had serious thoughts about teachin high school. Thought I could teach history and coach a little. I was gonna go to city college but we had Brandon and I had to start makin some money, so you know...

HERMAN. *(cont.)* But I like what I do. I own my own cab. See different parts of the city on a daily basis. Meet all types of interestin people, like your mother here, for instance.

(pause)

So how about some of this Chinese food.

*(**MARYANNE** suddenly goes to a knee, drops her cup of champagne. It spills everywhere.)*

DENNIS. Ma…

(She is somehow stuck, in severe pain.)

DENNIS. Ma, you okay?

HERMAN. Your ankle?

*(**HERMAN** moves to help her.)*

MARYANNE. I'm okay, I'm just…

*(**HERMAN** stops.)*

DENNIS. Mom, should I get –

MARYANNE. No, Dennis, just let me sit for a minute, I'll be fine.

(She takes a breath, then screams out.)

HERMAN. Maryanne –

DENNIS. I got it.

*(**DENNIS** helps her up.)*

DENNIS. Let's go to the bathroom, okay?

*(**DENNIS** carries **MARYANNE** to the bathroom, shuts the door. The bathroom radio is turned on. **DENNIS** and **MARYANNE**'s voices can be heard intensely discussing something, although it isn't discernable. **HERMAN** stands there for a moment, not sure what to do, then takes tissue and cleans up the spilled champagne. From the bathroom, two sharp cries. **HERMAN** freezes.)*

HERMAN. Everything okay in there?

*(No answer. Only the radio. **HERMAN** continues setting the food on the **DENNIS** enters from the bathroom.)*

HERMAN. Is it her ankle? I could rush her down to St. Vincent's in no time at all.

DENNIS. It's not her ankle. She's sick.

HERMAN. She caught a bug or somethin? Sometimes flyin'll do it to you. I can't tell you how many people I pick up from the airports who catch cold on the plane. Coughin, snifflin, carryin on. That's the main reason why I don't fly. Too many germs.

DENNIS. She's not sick from flyin.

HERMAN. She's like *sick* sick?

DENNIS. She has cancer.

HERMAN. Oh.

MARYANN. *(from the bathroom, over the music)* I'm okay, Herman. I'll just be a minute.

DENNIS. There was a tumor attached to one of her adrenal glands. It burst and seeded all throughout her hip and stomach and it spread pretty fast. About a month ago it got into her lungs.

HERMAN. Jesus.

DENNIS. She shouldn't have gone out tonight. Her doctor didn't even want her to take this trip.

HERMAN. How long does she have?

DENNIS. Maybe a month. Maybe less. She's sposed to be in hospice care. At home they just fixed her room up. The day before we flew out her I had to meet with the nurses and get like de-briefed about the trip. Like how to set up the orthopedic stuff in the bathroom and give her her pain medication and who to call if she got into a crisis.

HERMAN. I'm so sorry to hear all of this, Dennis. It must be awfully hard on you.

DENNIS. I just thought you should know.

HERMAN. Of course.

DENNIS. I mean, you can totally stay if you want, but...

HERMAN. I understand.

(bathroom radio ceases)

HERMAN. Is there a soda machine around here? I'm not sure champagne and Chinese food is such a good combination.

DENNIS. There's a Coke machine down the hall, just past the elevators.

HERMAN. I'm gonna go get some sodas. Be right back.

(HERMAN exits. DENNIS spots MARYANNE's baby blue windbreaker, takes it, examines it, hangs it up in the closet.)

(MARYANNE enters from the bathroom, looking worse.)

MARYANNE. Where'd he go?

DENNIS. To get some pop down the hall.

MARYANNE. Did you tell him?

DENNIS. No.

MARYANNE. Dennis…

DENNIS. I told him you caught a bug on the plane.

MARYANNE. You swear?

DENNIS. I swear.

MARYANNE. I just want to have this one nice night. Just this once, okay?

DENNIS. Okay. Should I call Dr. Baron?

MARYANNE. No.

DENNIS. Ma, he said –

MARYANNE. No Dr. Baron. Not tonight.

(A knock at the door. DENNIS crosses to it, opens the door. HERMAN enters holding a handful of sodas. He seems a bit stunned.)

HERMAN. Got some sodas.

(He stands there for a moment, confused.)

MARYANNE. Is something wrong, Herman?

HERMAN. Fella down by the ice machine said they just found a man on the fifteenth floor.

MARYANNE. A man? What man?

HERMAN. I mean his body. They found his body.

MARYANNE. Has someone been injured?

HERMAN. Fella at the ice machine said he was strangled to death. Apparently the whole lobby is fulla police.

MARYANNE. Oh my god. I'm so sorry you had to hear that news, Herman. On top of my shenanigans. Talk about a wet blanket.

HERMAN. It's no problem, Maryanne. No problem at all.

DENNIS. *(to* HERMAN*)* You sure he's dead? The guy downstairs?

HERMAN. That's what the man at the ice machine said.

*(*DENNIS *has somehow faded off.)*

MARYANNE. Denis...Dennis, you okay?

DENNIS. I'm fine.

*(*MARYANNE *moves to* DENNIS. DENNIS *crosses to the window, parts the curtains, looks down at the street.)*

MARYANNE. *(to* HERMAN*)* I think this city scares him a bit.

HERMAN. Maryanne, if you're not feelin well, I should prolly go.

MARYANNE. Oh. Okay...You sure I can't give you some money for the food?

HERMAN. It was my pleasure, really.

MARYANNE. I feel like I ruined such a nice night.

HERMAN. It's okay, Maryanne. It's really okay. You didn't ruin anything. You feel better.

MARYANNE. You still wanna go up to The Cloisters tomorrow?

HERMAN. Sure.

MARYANNE. What time?

HERMAN. How bout I call you here at the hotel? We'll make a plan then.

MARYANNE. Okay. Sounds good.

HERMAN. I had a really nice time tonight.

MARYANNE. I did, too, Herman.

HERMAN. Thank you again for the ticket.

MARYANNE. It was my pleasure, it really was.

*(**HERMAN** sets the Cokes on the table.)*

HERMAN. Nice to meet you, Dennis.

DENNIS. You, too.

HERMAN. Maryanne, you're a lovely woman.

(They hug chastely. She holds on a bit longer, then releases.)

*(He exits. **MARYANNE** sits on the end of one of the beds, starts to cry.)*

DENNIS. Ma...

(She cries.)

DENNIS. Ma, please don't cry.

(He goes to his knees, buries his head in her lap.)

MARYANNE. I'm so tired of this, Dennis. So sick and tired of the pain. And I'm tryin so hard to not feel sorry for myself. And I hate draggin you through this, I really do...I love you so much, Dennis. You're all I got left, you know?

(He nods.)

MARYANNE. I really wanted this trip to be fun for us. I'm sorry I tried to force that play on you...I just wanted us to have a nice time, you know...I really don't know how much longer I can stand this.

DENNIS. It's okay, Ma. Everything's gonna be okay.

MARYANNE. Thanks, sweetheart. You're such a brave guy. So brave.

DENNIS. You want the stronger stuff?

(She nods. He rises, crosses to the bathroom, returns with a different bottle of pills from before, hands them to her with a cup of water.)

DENNIS. Take an extra one tonight.

(She nods, takes the pills, drinks the water.)

MARYANNE. I need to lay down. Will you help me?

(He helps her up from the bed, leads her to the head of the other bed, pulls the blankets and sheets back, helps her undress, crosses to the bathroom, retrieves her night-gown, crosses back, helps her remove her bra and eases the nightgown over her head.)

MARYANNE. I'm freezing. Is there any way you can turn the heat up?

(He crosses to the thermostat, adjusts it. She gets into bed. He crosses to her, sits beside her.)

MARYANNE. Hey, you.

DENNIS. Hey.

MARYANNE. I used to think you looked like your father but I think you're startin to favor your Grandpa Shoe. Handsome guy.

(They just stare at each other.)

MARYANNE. Touch my head.

(He does so.)

MARYANNE. I love it when you touch my head.

(He gently strokes her hair, curls it behind her ears.)

MARYANNE. That Herman is such a nice man, isn't he? Really kind, you know?

(DENNIS nods.)

MARYANNE. *(laughing)* I wonder what your father would think. Me datin a black guy.

(She starts to hum a song from the play she saw.)

MARYANNE. Man, that girl in the play was so pretty. The best part of it was when they sang her pain away. Because she was sick, too, you know? She was so sick but they just sang it away, Dennis. It was really beautiful.

(She continues humming for a while, the pain killers taking effect, she falls asleep.)

(DENNIS starts to reach toward her, as if to touch her face, pulls his hand back, starts to cry, swallows all sound. His body contorts from suppressing it.)

(The sound of a cell phone. DENNIS looks to the table, confused, crosses to the table, searches among the Chinese takeout, retrieves it, realizes that it's FRANCES', puts it in his pocket.)

(DENNIS turns to MARYANNE, watches her. After a moment he grabs a pillow from the other bed, holds it severely.)

DENNIS. Ma… Ma…

(She wakes. He hesitates, then sets the pillow under her head. She reaches up and touches his face, draws her hand back, again sleeps.)

(He watches her breathe for a moment, crosses to the window, opens the drapes a bit. It is snowing.)

(He crosses back to her bed, stands over her, and removes the hammer, which is hidden in his waistband.)

DENNIS. *(whispering)* Ma… Ma, it's snowin.

(He continues to stand over her with the hammer as lights fade to black.)

From the Reviews of
KINDNESS...

"Compelling. A well-crafted mini-thriller, which keeps you in suspense until the final blackout."
– Joe Dziemianowics, *New York Daily News*

"Rapp has raised some provocative questions about the prickly mother/son relationship he has drawn in such detail."
– Marilyn Stasio, *Variety*

"Pungent, vivid...Rapp finds a gentle approach to his characters' physical and emotional pain without turning sentimental. His playful side is on display too." [Four stars]
– Diane Snyder, *Time Out New York*

"Adam Rapp can write dense, tense, funny dialogue."
– Charles Isherwood, *The New York Times*

"A taut and involving dark comedy. Hilarious and unsettling."
– Dan Bacalzo, *TheatreMania.com*

OTHER TITLES AVAILABLE FROM SAMUEL FRENCH

SIXTY MILES TO SILVER LAKE

Dan LeFranc

Dramatic Comedy / 2m

A moving car. A father and son. The father drives. The son's face is pressed against the rolled up window.

A lifetime can pass in the sixty miles between a boy's soccer practice and his father's new apartment. In this moving play about family relationships, we see just how much time and space can exist between the pleather seats of a father's used car.

"Nothing – and everything – happens in the hourlong car ride on a California highway depicted by Dan LeFranc in *Sixty Miles to Silver Lake.* Time marches onward (and jumps backward) in this painfully honest two-hander about the fragile relationship between a divorced dad and the son he picks up every Saturday after soccer practice and drives to his home for the weekend. But to this alienated pair, it's one endless ritual of loving and hating and hurting."
- *Variety*

"Dan LeFranc captures the conversational awkwardness, intimacy, and anger shared by a divorced man and his teenage son in *Sixty Miles to Silver Lake,* a poetic play in which bends in the road are the rule."
- *Backstage.com*